HEIDI HECKELBECK

Says "Cheese!"

By Wanda Coven
Illustrated by Priscilla Burris

LITTLE SIMON

New York London Toronto Sydney New Delhi

LITTLE SIMON
An imprint of Simon & Schuster Children's Publishing Division
1230 Avenue of the Americas, New York, New York 10020
First Little Simon paperback edition July 2015
Copyright © 2015 by Simon & Schuster, Inc.
Also available in a Little Simon hardcover edition.
All rights reserved, including the right of reproduction in whole or in part in any form. LITTLE SIMON is a registered trademark of Simon & Schuster, Inc., and associated colophon is a trademark of Simon & Schuster, Inc. For information about special discounts for bulk purchases, please contact Simon & Schuster Special Sales at 1-866-506-1949 or business@simonandschuster.com. The Simon & Schuster Speakers Bureau can bring authors to your live event. For more information or to book an event contact the Simon & Schuster Speakers Bureau at 1-866-248-3049 or visit our website at www.simonspeakers.com.
Designed by Ciara Gay
Manufactured in the United States of America 0119 MTN
10 9 8 7 6 5
Library of Congress Cataloging-in-Publication Data
Coven, Wanda.
Heidi Heckelbeck says "cheese!" / by Wanda Coven ; illustrated by Priscilla Burris.
pages cm
Summary: Distraught when her loose tooth falls out before Student Picture Day, second-grader Heidi Heckelbeck turns to her *Book of Spells* for a remedy.
ISBN 978-1-4814-2327-4 (pbk : alk. paper) — ISBN 978-1-4814-2328-1 (hc : alk. paper) — ISBN 978-1-4814-2329-8 (eBook) [1. Witches—Fiction. 2. Magic—Fiction. 3. Teeth—Fiction.] I. Burris, Priscilla, illustrator. II. Title.
PZ7.C83393Hm 2015
[Fic]—dc23
2014021870

CONTENTS

Chapter 1

TOOTH TROUBLE

Wiggle!

Jiggle!

Jaggle!

Heidi stood on a kitchen chair and looked in the mirror that hung by the back door. Mom used this mirror to put on lipstick before she left the house. Heidi used it to look at her loose tooth.

"Oh no!" she exclaimed. "That tooth is SUPER-loose!"

"Which one is it?" asked Mom.

Heidi turned around on the chair and put her finger on her tooth. "My *fwunt* one!" she said.

She wiggled it again.

"Wow, that *is* really loose," agreed Mom.

"Well, it had better not fall out!" declared Heidi.

Mom looked puzzled. "Why not?"

"Because Picture Day at school is in TWO days," Heidi said. "And I don't want a big hole in my smile."

"Then stop wiggling it," suggested Mom.

"That's easy for you to say!" Heidi
said, poking her tooth with her tongue.

"Get your mind on something else,"
said Mom.

Heidi tried to think about something else. She looked at the ceiling and rubbed her chin thoughtfully. Then she sighed.

"It's no use," she said. "All I can think about is my loose tooth."

"Well, I have an idea," said Mom. "Let's practice your spelling words."

Heidi groaned. "Do I have to?"

"It might get your mind off your tooth," Mom said.

"Well . . . okay," grumbled Heidi, hopping down from the chair.

Then she pulled her spelling words from the inside pocket of her note-book and handed them to Mom.

Mom looked over the list. "Words that begin with the letter *T*," she said as she sat on the couch. "Ready?"

Heidi nodded.

"Treat," said Mom.

"Treat," repeated Heidi. "T-R-E-A-T."

She clasped her hands behind her back and rocked back and forth on her heels as she spelled.

"Good," Mom said. "Toad."

"That's easy!" Heidi said. "T-O-A-D."

Mom nodded. "Tooth," she said.

As soon as Heidi heard the word "tooth," her tongue went straight to her loose tooth. Then she hopped back onto the chair and looked at her tooth in the mirror.

Mom sighed and laid the spelling words on the table.

Chapter 2

PiRATES AND WiTCHES

"We're home!" Henry shouted as he burst through the back door.

Henry had on a baseball cap and glove. When he saw Heidi standing on the chair, he stopped. Dad, who was right behind Henry, stopped to look at Heidi too.

"What are you doing?" asked Henry.

Heidi kept staring at herself in the mirror.

Mom filled them in. "Heidi has a loose tooth," she said.

"Wow, let me see!" said Henry, tossing his baseball glove into the sports bin.

Heidi shut her mouth and scowled.

"NO!" she said firmly. "Nobody gets
to see but ME."

"Why not?" asked Henry.

"Because if you look at my tooth,

it might fall out," said Heidi. "And it can't fall out before Wednesday."

"Why Wednesday?" questioned Henry.

"BECAUSE!" Heidi said. "Wednesday is Picture Day!"

"So?" said Henry.

"So I don't want my school picture taken if I have a MISSING TOOTH!" said Heidi angrily.

"Hmm . . . pirates have missing teeth," said Henry.

Heidi rolled her eyes. "Well, I'm not a pirate," she said. "I'm a WITCH!"

"Witches have missing teeth too," Henry said with a smile.

"Yeah, and you know what?" asked Heidi.

"What?" Henry answered.

"They look BEASTLY!" yelled Heidi. "That's what!"

Chapter 3

SKIP IT!

The next day Heidi's teacher Mrs. Welli reminded the class about Picture Day.

"We'll take individual pictures first," said Mrs. Welli. "Then we'll gather in the library for a class picture. Any questions?"

"May we stand next to our friends?"

asked Melanie Maplethorpe, who was
Heidi's least favorite girl in the class.

Mrs. Welli sighed.

"I can't make any promises," she
said. "Let's leave that to Mr. Horner."

Flash Horner was the
school photographer.

"Remember to bring
in your picture order

forms tomorrow. Or have your mom or dad sign up online," Mrs. Welli said. "I'll remind you again at the end of the day."

The lunch bell rang. Heidi and Lucy grabbed their lunch boxes and lined up for the cafeteria. Sometimes they got hot lunches, but most of the time they brought their own.

"So, what are you going to wear for Picture Day?" asked Lucy.

"I dunno," said Heidi. "What about you?"

"I'm going to wear my long-sleeved purple T-shirt with my pink skirt and purple flats," Lucy said.

Before Heidi could comment, Melanie butted in.

"Guess what I'M going to wear," she said loudly.

"Let me think," said Lucy. "Something pink?"

"And with ruffles?" added Heidi.

"Yes, but it's a whole NEW outfit," bragged Melanie. "The top is light pink with crisscross straps in the back, and the skirt is a darker pink with three layers of ruffles. And PS, it TWIRLS."

"Don't you have lots of outfits like that?" questioned Lucy.

"No, this one will be completely different," Melanie insisted. "You'll see." Then she turned to Heidi. "What are YOU going to wear? One of your weird tomboy outfits?"

Heidi gripped her lunch box. "That's my own personal business," she said.

Melanie stuck her nose in the air and walked off. Her pretty blond ponytail bobbed up and down as she went.

Heidi shook her head. Melanie drove her crazy, and all this talk

about Picture Day outfits made her think about her loose tooth again. She poked her tooth with the tip of her tongue. It felt looser than the last time she had checked.

Lucy noticed the worried look on Heidi's face. "What's the matter?" she asked.

"It's my dumb tooth!" Heidi said. "I don't want it to fall out before Picture Day!"

Heidi showed Lucy her loose tooth.

"It's loose, all right," said Lucy.

"What should I do?" asked Heidi.

Lucy thought for a moment. "Skip lunch," she said. "If you don't chew, maybe you won't lose your tooth!"

Heidi's face brightened.

"You're a GENIUS!" she said.

"Anytime," said Lucy.

Chapter 4

PLiNK!

Gurgle!

Gurgle!

Gur-r-r-r-p!

Heidi's stomach rumbled. She tried to ignore it, but it was hard to think about double-digit subtraction on an empty stomach. *Only half an hour*

until the bell rings, she thought. She watched Mrs. Welli write on the interactive board. But this time it wasn't a subtraction problem. It was a message. It said *Happy birthday, Natalie!* in great big letters.

"Time to hand out your birthday treats, Natalie," said Mrs. Welli.

Natalie went to the front of the room to get her box of treats. Everyone began to chatter.

"What treat?" asked Eve.

"Can I have some?" asked Charlie.

"Does it have nuts?" asked Melanie. "I can't have nuts."

"I hope it's cupcakes!" said Bruce.

Natalie picked Lucy to help pass out birthday napkins. Lucy placed a napkin on everyone's desk, and Natalie set an oatmeal chocolate

chip cookie on top of
each napkin. Bruce
was the first one
to take a bite of
his cookie.

"*Mmmmmm,*" he
moaned. "It . . . is . . .
SO good!"

Everyone made
some super-duper
yummy sounds—
everyone except
Heidi. She stared
at the cookie on
her desk. Her

stomach growled again. *Maybe if I just bite it gently,* Heidi said to herself. She picked up the cookie and bit into it softly, but even that was too much.

"OUCH!" yelped Heidi.

The bite of cookie dropped onto her desk.

Melanie, who sat next to her, saw

what happened. "EW!" she cried. "That's so GROSS!"

Everyone turned to look at Heidi. Her tooth was bent at an awkward angle.

Her classmates began to shout.

"Twist it!" exclaimed Charlie.

"Pull it!" cried Bruce.

"Tie it to a doorknob!" suggested Eve.

Heidi touched her tooth with her finger. She tried to push it back into place, but it was no use.

Plink!

Her front tooth dropped onto her desk—right next to the bite of cookie.

And just like that, it was all over.

Chapter 5

MRS. FOSTER

Heidi sat on the cot in the nurse's office. Mrs. Foster, the school nurse, had shoulder-length hair just like Heidi. She had on a pink turtleneck sweater, jeans, and short brown cowboy boots. Mrs. Foster handed Heidi a tissue and a handheld mirror.

"How's my twin?" she asked cheerily. Mrs. Foster always called Heidi her twin because they both had exactly the same color red hair.

Heidi shrugged and looked in the mirror. *Ugh,* she thought, frowning. *I look even worse than I thought.*

"You've got quite a gap there!" said Mrs. Foster.

"Merg," growled Heidi as she frowned at her reflection.

"Don't worry, sweetie. Everyone

loses teeth in second grade," said Mrs.
Foster. "It's part of growing up."

Then she opened a small refrigerator and pulled out a smiley-face ice pack.

"Maybe this will help," she said, handing the ice pack to Heidi.

"No, thank you," Heidi said. "I don't need an ice pack; I need a MIRACLE."

Mrs. Foster looked at Heidi thoughtfully. "What's the matter?" she asked. "Did you swallow your tooth?"

Heidi shook her head.

"Do you still have your lost tooth?" asked Mrs. Foster.

Heidi nodded. "It's in my hand," she said.

"May I see?" asked Mrs. Foster.

Heidi opened her hand to show Mrs. Foster her tooth. The tooth had a little hole where the root used to

be. This gave Heidi an idea.

"Can you glue my tooth back into place?" she asked hopefully.

Mrs. Foster wrinkled her forehead. "Why would you want me to do that?" she asked.

"Because tomorrow is Picture Day," said Heidi, "and I don't want to look like a jack-o'-lantern with a missing tooth!"

"Is that what this is all about?" asked Mrs. Foster as she sat down.

Heidi nodded and looked at her sneakers.

"Would it help if I said that you look adorable without your front tooth?" Mrs. Foster asked.

"Not really," mumbled Heidi, and she peeked in the mirror again. "What did you look like in second grade?" she asked.

Mrs. Foster laughed. "I had pigtails, glasses, and a half-grown-in front tooth," she said.

"Did you look absolutely adorable?" Heidi asked.

"I sure did!" said Mrs. Foster.

Heidi managed a weak smile.

"Okay, missy. May I borrow your
tooth?" asked Mrs. Foster.

Heidi carefully placed her tooth in
the school nurse's hand.

Then Mrs. Foster put the tooth in a tiny plastic container shaped like a tooth. She snapped the lid shut and handed it to Heidi.

The tooth holder had a purple string attached to the back so that it could be worn as a necklace. Heidi slipped the necklace over her head. *Well, at least I can wear my tooth around my neck,* she thought. Then she opened the tooth holder and looked at her tooth. *But I'd much rather have it back in my mouth, where it belongs.*

Chapter 6

FUNNY FACES

Heidi walked through the door and dropped her backpack beside the kitchen table. Henry was about to bite into a mini bagel with tomato sauce and melted cheese on top. But then he stopped and looked at his sister.

"What's wrong now?" he asked.

"My tooth fell out," Heidi said crossly.

"Cool!" exclaimed Henry. "Was there any blood?"

Heidi looked at Henry in disbelief. "What are you—a vampire or something?"

"Maybe," Henry said as he raised his arms like bat wings and stuck his front teeth out like fangs. "I vant to suck your blood!" he chanted.

Aunt Trudy and

Mom, who had been making more bagel snacks and lemonade, came over to the table.

"Okay, Heidi," said Aunt Trudy. "Open up!"

"Let's see your new smile!" chimed in Mom.

"No!" said Heidi firmly. "It looks SO BEASTLY."

"Beastly" had become her new favorite word.

"Come on. Just show us!" urged Henry. "What's the big deal?"

Heidi glared at her brother. Then she growled and showed her teeth like an angry dog. "There!" she declared. "Now everyone knows how beastly I look."

Mom raised her hands to her cheeks. "You look so adorable!" she exclaimed.

"Sweet as pie!" said Aunt Trudy.

"BEASTLY!" said Henry.

"Bingo!" said Heidi, folding her arms. "For once Henry is right!"

"Okay, that's enough, you two," said Mom.

"But Heidi should be happy," said

Henry. "Now she'll get a present from the tooth fairy!"

"I would much rather have a tooth than get a visit from the tooth fairy," said Heidi.

Then she planted her elbows on the table and rested her chin on her hands. Normally, she loved getting stuff from the tooth fairy, but this time all she could think about was how awful she was going to look in her school picture.

"Grrrr," growled Heidi again. "Why did I have to lose my tooth right before Picture Day?"

"Nobody says you have to show your teeth when you smile," said Henry. "Do a lips-only smile."

"Henry's right," said Mom. "Why don't you practice a new smile for Picture Day?"

Heidi stared blankly into space. *Maybe they are right,* she thought. *I suppose I COULD try another type of smile.* She got up and dragged her chair over to the back-door mirror. Then she began to practice some new smiles.

First she smiled with her lips only. *Ugh. No way,* she thought. *That doesn't look natural.* Then she tried her normal smile—just to see. *Ack!* she thought, and made a sour face.

This triggered an angry face, followed by . . .

A sad face.

A crazy face.

And a fish face.

Then Heidi stuck out her tongue
and made a big, fat growl sound.

RAWRRRR!

Chapter 7

MOM'S SURPRISE

"There's my beautiful girl!" Dad said as he walked through the back door from work.

Dad had seen Heidi's funny face show from the mudroom. He lifted Heidi from the chair and gave her a great big hug and a kiss on the nose.

"I look like a storybook witch," Heidi said glumly.

"She's a toothless old witch!" added Henry.

"And I feel beastly!" said Heidi.

"She is a BEAST!" Henry declared.

Heidi nodded. "It's true," she said.

Dad squeezed Heidi and laughed. "Then you're the prettiest beastly old witch I've ever seen!" he said as he let Heidi slide to the floor.

Mom walked over and bent down to put her arm around Heidi. "Cheer up," she said. "I have something that will make you feel better about Picture Day."

Heidi gave her mom a questioning look. *What could Mom possibly have that will make me feel better?* she wondered.

Mom beckoned Heidi with her finger. Heidi slowly followed her into the front hall. They walked upstairs and into Heidi's bedroom. There, on the bed, lay a brand-new outfit.

Heidi gasped.

"I decorated the skirt myself," Mom said.

It was a blue denim skirt with little stars sewn in colorful thread all over it. Mom had bought a light green top to go with it.

"I LOVE it!" Heidi said, forgetting her toothless self for a moment.

Mom smiled.

"Can I wear my jean jacket with it?" Heidi asked.

Mom nodded happily. "Of course you can," she said. "That'll give it the classic Heidi style."

Heidi picked up the hangers and held up the clothes against herself.

"They will look beautiful on you," said Mom. Then

she looked at her watch. "I have to go make dinner," she said. "But why don't you come down and model your new outfit for us?"

Heidi nodded as Mom left the room. Then she held her new outfit up to herself in front of the mirror.

She tilted her head from one side to the other. *This is my new favorite skirt,* she said to herself.

Then she smiled and saw the gap in her teeth again. *Ugh,* she thought. *My smile ruins the WHOLE outfit!*

Chapter 8

MiNi MARSH- MALLOWS

No way!

No how!

No chance!

I am NOT having my picture taken with my front tooth missing! Heidi thought. *And that's final!* Then she did what any witch her age would do. She pulled out her *Book of Spells*, along with her Witches of Westwick medallion. Then she opened to the Contents page and found a section called Spells for Teeth.

Heidi ran her finger down the chapter headings: Treating Toothaches. How to Straighten Teeth. How to Replace a Missing Tooth. *That's it!* Heidi thought. She fluttered the pages to the right chapter. Then she read the spell.

How to Replace a Missing Tooth

Are you a witch with a missing tooth? Perhaps you think toothless witches belong only in fairy tales. Would you like to look like a more fashionable, up-to-date witch? Then this is the spell for you!

Ingredients:

1 mini marshmallow

1/2 cup of water

1/4 teaspoon of lemon juice

a pinch of brown sugar

Mix the water, juice, and sugar together in a glass. Hold your Witches of Westwick medallion in one hand, and place your other hand over the glass. Chant the following spell:

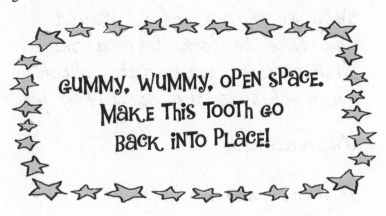

GUMMY, WUMMY, OPEN SPACE.
MAKE THIS TOOTH GO
BACK INTO PLACE!

Drink the mix and eat the marshmallow. In a few moments your tooth will be firmly back in its place.

Heidi took a deep breath and bit her lip. *We'd better have mini marsh-mallows!* she thought.

Chapter 9

LITTLE MISS GRIN

Heidi slipped into her pajamas and cracked open her bedroom door. Henry had already been tucked in, and Mom had gone into her office. Dad was in his lab.

Heidi quietly snuck downstairs to the kitchen. She found regular-size marshmallows in the pantry. *Maybe I can snip these into smaller pieces,* she thought. She pulled a handful of marshmallows from the bag. Then she quickly measured out the rest of the spell ingredients into a glass.

Heidi was just
about to leave the kitchen
when she heard the lab door squeak
open. *It's DAD!* she thought. She
dashed past Mom's office and bolted
up the stairs.

Heidi heard Dad's footsteps on the stairs. She ducked into her room and closed the door. She quickly set the glass and the marshmallows on her desk. Her heart pounded as she waited for her father to pass by her room. But the footsteps stopped at her door! Heidi held her breath. Dad opened the door.

"What's going on?" he asked as he looked at the marshmallows, the glass, the *Book of Spells*, and the Witches of Westwick medallion on Heidi's desk.

Heidi bit her lip. She was SO busted.

"I was going to use a spell to put my

tooth back in place," she mumbled.

Dad shook his head and sighed. "We'll have none of that," he said. "Come with me. I want to show you something."

Heidi slowly got up and followed her dad into her parents' bedroom.

Dad slid an old photo album down from the top shelf in his closet. He wiped the dust from the cover with the back of his hand.

Then Dad sat down on the bed. Heidi plunked down next to him. Dad opened the album. There were pictures of him as a baby, a toddler, and a little kid.

"And here's my second-grade picture," said Dad as he turned the page.

Heidi couldn't believe it. There was Dad with not one, but *two* missing front teeth. He had on the biggest smile ever.

"I was all gums," Dad said proudly.

"Wow," said Heidi. "You had it BAD."

"My mom called me Mr. Grin," said Dad.

Heidi laughed as Dad turned the page.

"Here's Mr. Grin on his bike, Mr. Grin

playing baseball, Mr. Grin up a tree, and Mr. Grin with his best friend," Dad went on.

"You look like you're having fun," Heidi said.

"I *was!*" said Dad. "And I'm having just as much fun looking back on it." Then Dad put his arm around Heidi. "And you can have fun with your missing tooth too," he said. "It happens. Just *own* it."

Heidi liked the way her dad looked in the pictures. He was having a lot more fun than she was.

She looked up at her dad and smiled. "Okay," Heidi said. "I'll give it a try."

"Now, that sounds more like my Heidi," said Dad, giving her a squeeze. Then he walked her back to her

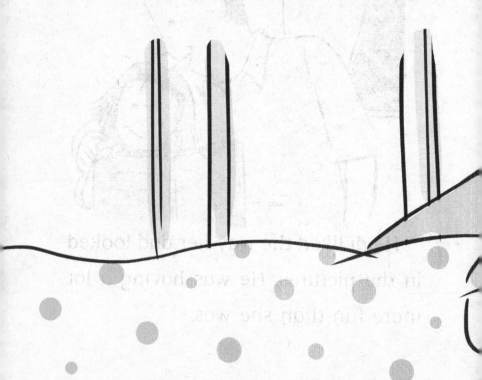

room. Heidi crawled under her covers and put her tooth on her bedside
table. Dad kissed her forehead.

"Good night, Little Miss Grin," he
said.

Chapter 10

JUST OWN IT!

Heidi found a brand-new purple headband under her pillow in the morning from the tooth fairy. It had colorful stars sewn on it—just like the ones on her new skirt. Heidi put on her Picture Day outfit and matching headband. She also slipped on her

tooth holder necklace. She smiled at herself in the mirror.

"Just own it!" she said to herself.

Then she hurried downstairs, ate a chocolate chip waffle, and headed for the bus with Henry. Henry had on a new striped polo shirt for Picture Day.

At school Heidi's class lined up for individual pictures. The children combed their hair and talked in line.

"Should I wear my glasses?" Lucy asked Heidi.

"Definitely," Heidi replied. "They're super-stylish and so YOU."

"Thanks," said Lucy. "Are you feeling better about your lost tooth?"

"Much better," Heidi said. "By the way, do I have any waffle in my teeth?"

Lucy inspected Heidi's teeth. "You're good," she said.

Then Heidi checked Lucy's teeth. "You're good too," said Heidi.

Smell-a-nie dashed past with a sparkly compact mirror in one hand and strawberry lip balm in the other.

She looked at Heidi and nodded.
"Nice skirt, WEIRDO," Melanie said as
she cut in line next to Stanley.

Heidi looked at Lucy.

"I think that was meant to be a
compliment," whispered Lucy.

"Minus the 'weirdo' part," Heidi
whispered back.

The girls giggled and inched ahead in line.

"How are you going to smile?" asked Lucy. "Teeth showing or *NOT* showing?"

"Teeth show-ing," said Heidi. "Definitely!"

"Me too," Lucy said.

"The only problem is, it's hard to smile when everyone's staring at you," Heidi said.

"You're not kidding," said Lucy. "Let's come up with something funny to think about when it's our turn."

"Okay," said Heidi.

The girls looked at each other and tried to think of something funny.

"I know!" said Lucy. "How about that time you did a split in the gym and ripped a huge hole in your pants?"

"That was so NOT funny," said Heidi. "You could see my flower underwear!"

Lucy laughed. "That was the best part!" she said.

"Very funny," said Heidi. "How about the time you jumped off the swing and landed in a mud puddle?"

"But that hurt!" Lucy complained. "And I was COVERED in mud!"

"I know. It was hilarious!" said Heidi, cracking up.

Lucy frowned. "Okay, I'll think of that HUMONGOUS rip in your pants when it's my turn," she said. "And you can think of me covered in mud when it's your turn."

And when it was time to say "Cheese!" that's exactly what they did.

Chapter 11

FREEZE FRAME

Heidi, Lucy, and Henry waved their school picture packets as they charged into the kitchen. It had been a whole month since Picture Day. Heidi's new front tooth had already started to come in, and she had another loose tooth.

"We're HOME!" Heidi cried.

"No kidding!" said Mom, getting out of the way.

"The gang's all here!" said Dad, clapping his hands together.

"We got our pictures back!" Heidi announced as she hung up her jean jacket and backpack.

"So, how did they turn out?" asked
Mom.

"Good!" exclaimed the children.

"May we see them?" Dad asked.

"YES!" they exclaimed again.

Everyone sat at the kitchen table.
Heidi opened her pictures and laid

them out on the table. Mom and Dad looked them over.

"Now THAT'S a great smile," said Dad. "You look truly happy."

"I was!" Heidi said.

Then they looked at Henry's pictures. His shirt was buttoned all the way to the top, and he had smiled with all his might.

"Oh, my!" Mom said. "You look so grown-up!"

"My shirt is choking me," said Henry. "But it's not too bad."

Lucy laid out her pictures.

"Another winner!" said Dad. "How did you guys do it?"

"Easy," said Heidi. "Lucy and I just

thought of something funny before we had our pictures taken."

"What about you, Henry?" asked Dad.

"I just thought of Heidi," he said. "She always makes me crack up."

"Very funny," said Heidi.

"I have something for your pic-tures," Mom said.

She went to her office and came back with a small brown bag. She pulled out two picture frames. Then she trimmed a picture of Heidi and a picture of Henry and slid them into

the frames. Heidi and Lucy exchanged pictures of each other for their bulletin boards.

Then the girls sat down and discussed their class picture.

"Look at Melanie!" Lucy cried. "She made a mad face!"

"She can't help it!" said Heidi. "She's a meanie!"

Mom frowned. "That's not nice," she said.

The girls squealed with laughter.

"Look at Charlie," said Lucy. "He's totally squinting!"

"And Natalie wrinkled her nose!" Heidi said, pointing.

"It looks like she smelled a rotten egg!" said Lucy.

"She probably did!" Heidi agreed.

The girls shrieked with more laughter.

"Why is Bruce wearing his safety goggles?" asked Henry.

"Because he wouldn't be Bruce without them!" said Heidi.

"He's going to be a famous scientist one day," added Lucy.

"Look at Eve," said Lucy. "She's missing a tooth, like you!"

Heidi took a closer look. "Oh yeah!" she said. "But it's a bottom one. It hardly shows."

Dad looked over the girls' shoulders. "That's one good-looking class!" he remarked.

Heidi smiled. "Oh, no we're not!"

she joked. "We're super-BEASTLY!"

"But in a good way," said Lucy.

"In the very BEST way," added Heidi.

Check out the next book starring

HEIDI HECKELBECK

Might Be Afraid of the Dark

Click!

Click!

Click!

Heidi switched on three lights: The bedroom light, the bathroom light, and the hall light. Then she kicked off her slippers and hopped into bed.

"I'm ready!" she called.

An excerpt from *Heidi Heckelbeck Might Be Afraid of the Dark*

She listened to her mother's foot-steps as they came down the hall and into her room.

Her mom sighed.

"It looks like daytime when you go to bed," her mother said. "Let me turn off *one* of these lights."

Heidi shook her head firmly.

She always slept with three lights on. She also had two flashlights stashed in her nightstand—just in case the power went out.

"Nighttime is FRIGHT time!" she declared. Then she hid under the covers.

An excerpt from *Heidi Heckelbeck Might Be Afraid of the Dark*

Her mother frowned and shook her head. "Someday you'll think being afraid of the dark is silly," she said.

Heidi pulled the covers back down and put a finger on her lips. *"Shhhh!"* she shushed. "I don't want Henry to hear!"

"HEAR WHAT?" shouted Henry from across the hall. "That you're SCARED of the DARK?"

"AM NOT!" Heidi shouted back. "I just like to sleep with the lights on— that's all."

An excerpt from *Heidi Heckelbeck Might Be Afraid of the Dark*